BUTTERCUPS AND BETRAYAL

A TREEHOUSE HOTEL COZY MYSTERY (BOOK 3)

SUE HOLLOWELL

Buttercups and Betrayal

Copyright © 2020 by Sue Hollowell

Cover design by Donna L. Rogers dlrcoverdesigns.com

Editing by: Tiffany White at Writers Untapped

CONTENTS

CHAPTER ONE

Every light blazed in the normally dark Cedarbrook Historical Museum as Mom and I pulled into the parking lot. I maneuvered my car into a parking space as my mother eyed the bright, busy building from the passenger seat.

"They really pulled out all the stops tonight," she said, but the way she grumbled made it sound more like an insult than a compliment.

"Well, it's a big deal," I said, trying to keep the mood chipper. Mom had been critical of the museum's handling of the town history for a long time. "It's been a long time since we've added a new piece to our small-town collection."

I parked and helped her out of the car, and together, we walked to the front door. The two-story brick building was a historic landmark in the community, and had really been revitalized these last few years, especially recently with the appointment of a new curator. Tonight, the doors were propped open, and people milled about in the lobby, inspecting the displays and the buffet of hors d'oeuvres.

But Mom would not be sidetracked. She steered me through the double doors at the other end of the lobby and into the auditorium. Empty chairs lined the aisles. At the far end, a heavy, velvet curtain hid the new artifact from view. Much to Mom's dismay, it was guarded by Angela.

Angela wore a period costume, displaying a full-length, long-sleeved dress covered by a pinafore apron. Above her pioneer-woman boots I saw the ruffles of bloomers. And to top it off, she wore a prairie bonnet over her bright red hair.

"Hi Chloe, Mabel." She greeted us with hugs. Angela was married to my nephew at one point, and she stayed close to my sister through the years. Now, she was a supervisor here at the museum. It was the perfect position for her. She could recite the town history by heart and had endless stories about each piece owned by the museum.

"You won't let me get a peek, will you?" Mom asked, trying to lean around Angela. She was somewhat of a collector herself, hoarding several items in the hotel office that she refused to donate to the museum in spite of many valiant attempts by the staff through the years.

Angela laughed good-naturedly. "Unfortunately not, but here, these front-row seats are available. Best seats in the house."

We settled into the seats she offered.

"I'm going to go try to find Mr. Higgons so we can get started soon," Angela said. As she walked back up the aisle to hunt for the curator, her skirts swished around her ankles.

The seat beside me was quickly filled by a chubby woman with short, black hair carrying an over-sized, leopard-print purse. The woman leaned around me and greeted my mother.

"Mabel, good to see you here."

My mom gave her a cursory glance. "Donna." Then, to me, she said, "Chloe, this is Donna. She's on the board of the museum."

I shook Donna's hand. When she withdrew, she dug into her purse, extracting a butterscotch candy, which she offered to us. Mom declined, but I accepted her gift with thanks, if only not to be rude.

Donna looked around at the crowd. "Our little museum is really making a name for itself, don't you think? Bart Higgons has been just an invaluable addition to the team."

I glanced over my shoulder. "I think Angela went looking for him. We didn't see him when we came in."

Donna dismissed the comment with a wave of her hand. "He'll be here. It's a big day for him, after all."

But when I saw Angela hurrying down the aisle beside a severe-looking woman in a tailored pantsuit, I had my doubts. The woman climbed the stairs to the stage and took what was supposed to be Bart's place behind the podium. The crowd hushed as she began to speak, the microphone crackling a bit at first.

"Welcome, Cedarbrook. I'm Judy Livingston. Many of you may know me as the mayor of our little town."

As Judy paused while people clapped, Mom leaned around me to Donna. "What were you saying about Bart?"

Donna waved her away again.

The mayor continued, "I'm pleased to welcome you tonight to our growing little gem of a museum, putting us on the map of the national tour of museums. This is due, in no small part, to the stellar curator I hired to develop this place into an award-winning destination. At the moment, we are unable to locate Bart Higgons, so we'll begin the program."

Judy pulled a piece of paper from a folder and began reading. She described the new piece in the museum as the oldest-known functioning water canteen in existence from the pioneers exploring the west. She finished detailing the piece, handed her paper and folder to her assistant, and grabbed the cord to the curtain. She tugged on the heavy drape to slowly reveal the display in a dramatic fashion.

With a couple of tugs, the display was in full view.

And so was Bart Higgons's body on the floor in front of the bench.

Spotlights blazed over the scene. Gasps filled the room. Someone rushed forward to check Bart's pulse before looking up at Judy. "He's dead," he announced.

Beside me, Mom gasped and grabbed my hands, squeezing with her bony fingers. At the base of the stage, Angela clapped her hands over her mouth.

"Maybe we should go," I whispered to my mom.

"Not on your life," she bit back.

Judy rushed in. "The canteen's missing," she yelled. Then, seeming to realize her callous response, she tried to recover. "Poor Bart. And he was doing so well here. Who could do such a thing?"

Angela seemed to shake off her surprise and started taking charge. She gave two sharp claps of her hands to get the crowd's attention, and then started herding all the rubberneckers up the aisle and back to the lobby where they could gossip to their hearts' content until the police arrived. There would probably even be new arrivals once the news spread. The joys of small-town living.

I stood and helped Mom to her feet. Donna had already vacated the seat beside me and gathered with the small crowd around Bart's body.

My mom was handling things in her normal fashion, grumbling as she gathered her purse. "I came out for a nice evening," she said, "and now this." She gazed with disgust at the body on the stage.

For once, I agreed with her.

This was definitely not the night we had planned.

CHAPTER TWO

Mom and I were on our way out, bringing up the tail end of the crowd, when Angela returned, snagging me by my shoulder.

"Please don't leave," she whispered. "I can't deal with—" She stopped, her eyes going wide as she looked over my shoulder.

"Unbelievable," came Judy's sharp voice. We all turned to see her still on the stage, her wide, dark eyes narrowed on Angela. "I knew you'd make trouble if we didn't select you for the curator position."

Angela took a step back as if from the force of the accusation. "I did not!" she objected.

Judy, trailed by Donna, marched up the aisle. Trapped, I nudged Mom into one of the rows to get out of the way. From here, I could see sweat beading on Angela's brow, but I felt it was probably more thanks to the layers of heavy clothing she wore than to any guilty conscience.

Angela wasn't family anymore, but I knew her, and I knew she wasn't capable of murder.

At least, I thought she wasn't. She was singularly devoted to her daughter.

"Now, hold on just a minute," I interjected. "I think we need to call the Emerald Hills police and get them down here to do the investigating before we start pointing fingers."

But my objections fell on deaf ears. The mayor whirled on Donna, who held her leather bag in front of her like a shield. "And you. I had a feeling Bart was trouble, but you insisted on hiring him."

"I did no such thing," Donna objected. As she talked, the hard candy she sucked on clacked against her teeth. "You knew full well his background and the rumors about his shady dealings. Your decisions are always tainted by the almighty buck. All you could talk about was how Bart's museum expansion plans would bring more money in."

"Shady dealings?" my mom whispered to me.

I shrugged as Donna and Judy continued to trade jabs.

"When the museum board meets next week, I'll be petitioning to have you removed." Judy paced in front of the stage, Bart's body behind her, largely unacknowledged. "The only reason you're there is because you wormed your way in by saying you're a collector." Judy made air quotes around the word collector.

Donna shook her head and smirked. "You wouldn't know a historical collectible if it hit you over the head. At least I knew what Bart was talking about when he proposed acquiring new pieces."

The crowd was now long gone. The yelling echoed off the tall, exposed beam ceilings. With Judy and Donna going at each other, this seemed like the perfect time to make our escape. Slipping out of the row, I grabbed Angela's hand.

"Chloe, you've got to help me. I had nothing to do with this," Angela said. "If I lose this job, I'll never get my daughter back."

I placed my hand on Angela's back and softly said, "I'll do what I can." I looked over at the curtain. Someone had lowered it, disguising the evening's tragedy, but I knew the impact of the murder was just beginning.

As I ushered Mom and Angela from the room, Mom took up her grumbling again. "This is why I won't let the museum have any of my things. They tell me they care about the history, and then something like this happens."

I said goodbye to Angela, promising to help where I could, and opened the door for Mom to get into the car. By the time I sat down and started the car, I was exhausted. This was the type of night where I couldn't wait to hang out with my cuddly cocker spaniel and forget the craziness of the world for at least a few hours.

CHAPTER THREE

That night, after dropping Mom off, I made my way to the Buttercup Bungalow treehouse unit that had become our home over the last few months. It was technically part of the hotel my mom owned and had been the first room we'd decorated together. It looked like the home decor store had exploded in here, but I loved how bright and warm it was. It likely wasn't a permanent arrangement, but right now, the peace and tranquility of the forest was exactly what I needed.

Max and I snuggled up on the small loveseat in the front room, my huckleberry vodka cocktail and Max's ginger treats on the table, along with a new puzzle ready for solving.

I placed my feet on the ottoman, opened the puzzle book, and got out my pencil. Our puzzle preference was for numbers, not words. Not that I didn't like word search or a simple crossword, but my brain somehow gravitated toward the logic. Our new adventure tonight was a KenKen puzzle. It was similar to our usual sudoku but with the extra factor of computation. We'd start on an easy one until we learned the techniques to master the more complex.

The way this worked with Max was that I would read the clues out loud and he would tap on the page with his answer. I would confirm the number and he would shake his head yes or no. It was going to be fun to see how he did adding math to the picture.

I stroked his silky brown fur as I read the first clue. I always waited for him to answer first. After a long pause, he raised his paw, placed it on the book and looked at me, appearing unconfident in his answer. I hoped he didn't think I was trying to trick him.

I laughed. "You got it, boy," I said.

He smiled that mile-wide Muppet grin, pleased with his accomplishment.

I took a turn at the second clue. He watched me write the number in the book. When he saw what it was, he nodded his head. So much for the beginner level. As always, Max was a quick study.

I petted his head. "This isn't our only puzzle to solve. Somehow, Bart at the museum ended up dead on opening night of the reveal of the new collection. And the canteen is missing."

He stood and wagged his tail, always ready to tackle another mystery.

"Ah, not now. But I definitely need your help," I said.

He returned to his puzzle-solving position.

I read the next clue to him, he pointed to the number, and looked at me again. *Spot on, Max. We might have to go to the next level of difficulty right now.*

Max and I continued tag teaming the puzzle. We finished the first one and moved on to a second. He scooted closer to me, almost halfway into my lap. I took that as a sign that he liked the KenKen.

But I was distracted, the mystery of the murder weighing heavy on my mind, especially with Angela as a potential suspect.

"I know Bart was a divisive figure in this community, even though he'd only been in town less than a year," I said. "With that scene at the museum the night of the murder, I couldn't tell if Judy or Donna liked Bart or not. I think they liked what he did for the museum, but maybe not how he went about it." I looked down at Max, certain by now he understood my words. We had worked enough puzzles, including solving murders, that I knew we were in sync.

I leaned down and gave him a hug with my left arm. He was such a calming influence when needed.

"We're going to have to learn a little more about Bart. What do you say we start on that tomorrow?"

Max leapt up like he'd seen a bunny he wanted to chase. He barked once and wagged that stubby little tail so hard I thought it would fly off his body.

Just then, my phone vibrated. I picked it up off the table and studied the caller ID before answering. It was my sister, Angela's ex-mother-in-law. I was sure she'd heard everything by now.

I put the puzzle book and pencil on the table and answered the phone. "Hi, Joey. How are you holding up?"

"I'm just so worried about Angela," she said, starting right in. "She's almost inconsolable." Joey's normally freewheeling personality was now all business.

"I'm sorry, Joey. That has to be horrible for her. And for you," I added.

Angela had been married to my sister Joey's son, Brady, but it had been a tumultuous relationship, mostly because Brady always seemed to find trouble. They'd had a daughter together, Samantha, but Angela didn't currently have custody until she could move into a bigger place.

"She was on track to have Sam back in her home again. If she'd gotten the curator position, that would have given her enough money to get her own place," Joey said. "I just don't know what to do. Do you think you can help?"

Max put his chin on my thigh and gazed up at me, his large, brown eyes somber. Absently, I stroked his head. "I don't know a lot about Bart, but Max and I will ask around and see what we can do."

Joey's voice cracked. "I know it looks bad for her, but I'm sure Angela had nothing to do with Bart's death. She's a good mom to Sam and would never do anything to jeopardize getting her back."

"This won't be easy. I'll keep you posted," I said.

We exchanged our goodbyes and hung up. I returned the phone to the table and looked at Max. He ever so quietly whimpered, his jowls drooping.

"I agree. It's sad for so many reasons."

Max's eyes diverted to the table on my right and the plate of ginger treats. His gaze returned to mine, requesting permission to dig in. We needed to fuel up if we were moving full-on into murder-solving mode. I nodded my head. The predictability of his penchant toward ginger warmed my heart.

He stood and carefully tiptoed across my lap to retrieve a cookie. He snagged one, returned to his seat, and quietly munched. We both enjoyed our goodies and pondered our mission to find Bart's killer, locate the missing museum collectible, and clear Angela's name.

I placed the book of KenKen puzzles on the table, saving them for another day.

CHAPTER FOUR

The air had started to turn crisp in the mornings, hinting at fall. Mom and I were meeting Paul this morning at the hotel to do a walk-through of the initial construction plans for our expansion. The two new units and the lodge were the biggest changes that had happened to this place since it was initially built. Mom and I had been redecorating the existing units like crazy so we would be ready for the two new ones. Mom was pleased as punch that she got to name them. I was a bit hesitant, given how she could go a little sideways with things at times. But Crocus Castle and Dogwood Den fit perfectly with the theme of the existing treehouses. And Lily Lodge gave us so much potential for decorating ideas that we already had some of the curtains purchased.

I heard the crunch of gravel from the driveway and assumed that would be Paul, the construction manager for our project. Since my return to Cedarbrook, I had become reacquainted with many of the residents I knew from my youth and met quite a few new ones. Paul had come recommended from Pearl, where he had put in some upgrades at her Pearl's Pooch Pampering business.

I stood and peered through the small window. "Mom, I think Paul's here."

She was seated in a corner, flipping through a decorating magazine. She had acquired quite a stack of those in preparation for our new project. "OK, dear." She continued perusing with her head down.

"I think he wants us to walk around with him to tour the site where they'll be building." I tried to budge her from her focus. No luck.

"You can do that. You don't need me," she said.

I shrugged and opened the door to greet Paul. I didn't expect to see what I found on the other side. Paul was about six feet tall, cropped white hair, and a salt-and-pepper scruffy beard. He wore a plaid flannel shirt over heavy duty construction pants and work boots.

Mom bolted out of her chair like it had caught fire. She was at my side in about one-second flat, reaching out to shake his hand before he was even in the door. And Max was right behind her. You would think she had never seen a handsome man before.

"I'm Mabel, the owner of this hotel. Nice to meet you," she said.

He laughed, easing the awkward tension. "Hello, Mabel, nice to meet you as well."

I stepped away from the door to let him in. "Mom, why don't you let Paul in for a minute before we do our tour?" I said.

She let go of his hand and stepped to the side to make room for his entry. Taking her place in the doorway, Max stepped in to greet Paul. He bent over and gave Max a good scratch behind his ears. Max turned and bounded over to me, with obvious approval of Paul.

"That's quite the welcoming committee," Paul said, chuckling. "I think I'm going to really enjoy this project, for lots of reasons." Paul stepped inside, and I closed the door.

Mom eyeballed me behind Paul's back. I ignored her look. No way was I ready for a boyfriend. It didn't matter how handsome he was. I had a job to do. And when Max and I weren't busy at the hotel, we had a murder to solve.

"I've brought the plans with me, but I thought we could look at the site first to talk about how this is going to happen," Paul said. He set the large roll of architecture drawings on the guest registration desk.

Mom and Max returned to front and center, both of them with matching goofy grins on their faces. I avoided eye contact or I would've never been able to get through this.

"OK," I said. "Mom, let's get our coats and head out. We can talk about the decorations later."

She was as giddy as a schoolgirl. I knew how her mind worked. She already had Paul and me married. She practically skipped to get her jacket and followed us outside. Max galloped alongside us. I wasn't sure if it was because he got to go outside or he was happy to have a new friend, or both.

We traversed the path around the center firepit and gathering place, just beyond the Morning Glory Manor. I rubbed my arms to warm up.

Paul gestured to the open area just beyond the circle of units we currently had in operation. "This is where we're going to build Dogwood Den. We've got these two gorgeous pine trees situated in a way that we can incorporate both of them into the treehouse. One of them is in a position to be the center. And the second one is going to be the corner of the outside deck."

Mom, Max, and I craned our necks up to look in the direction Paul pointed toward the tops of the trees. This would be one of the tallest units and have one of the best views. Max and I might have to move here from the Buttercup Bungalow.

Paul continued the path about a hundred yards to the east where Crocus Castle would be.

I reached over to hold Mom's elbow. "Be careful with your step, Mom. It's starting to get a little slippery." For some reason, she wore shoes today that were good for traipsing through the woods. It was usually about what looked good rather than functionality.

Paul had stopped and waited for us. "This is Crocus Castle's new home." He beamed. "I can't wait to get started on these. It's going to be a fun project. Do you have any questions right now?"

I looked at Mom. That grin had returned to her face. I gave a small shake of my head, hoping Paul didn't notice. She would never stop being a matchmaker. "I don't think so. Let's head back inside and warm up with some coffee as we look over the plans."

We turned and retraced our steps back to the office. As we approached the door, I saw Max buried in a bush up to his rear, that stubby little tail practically spinning like a propeller. "C'mon, Max," I said and patted my leg. He didn't budge. If anything, his tail wagged faster. "Max!" Whatever had his attention must have been fascinating. He pulled his head out and looked at me. So many leaves were attached to his head it looked like he was wearing a crown. "Let's go inside." He relented, not wanting to leave his prey. The squirrels at the hotel had been more prevalent lately, appearing to be getting ready for winter. I thought they were taunting Max, but he had a ball chasing them as they escaped up the trees.

We got inside and I started a pot of coffee. Max fawned all over Paul, bonding with his new friend. Paul started picking the leaves from Max's fur. "That fur is like Velcro for sticks and leaves," he said.

I got three cups out and set them next to the coffee pot. "It's a constant battle," I said. "But well worth it for my buddy."

"So Paul, tell us about yourself." Mom put her jacket on the hook by the door.

Oh boy, here we go. I stepped over to the building plans and began unrolling the paper. "Mom, let's look over the plans while we wait for our coffee."

She shook her head. "Chloe, you don't have to be all business, all the time."

Paul came to the desk to wrangle the paper rolls and lay them out so we could see them. He looked up at me with those warm brown eyes. My face began to heat up. I grabbed the stapler to hold down one corner of the papers.

Paul pulled the reservation book over to weigh down the opposite side of the plans. "I can't tell you how much I appreciate your business too. This has been my dream for some time," he said.

"I'm glad it worked out for us too," Mom said and joined us at the desk. She looked at me and smiled, not disguising her intent one bit. I felt like my whole body would catch fire from the heat igniting inside of me. She and I were going to have a direct conversation after Paul left. No fixing me up.

"If I hadn't gotten your project, I'd likely have gone out of business. Or at least had to put a hold on things while I returned to my previous job as a delivery driver. Not that I didn't like it, but getting up at four o'clock every day wore me out," he said.

"I saw what you did at Pearl's. You do good work." My flushed cheeks remained. I really hoped he didn't notice. I wiped my clammy hands on my pants.

"It's just that the big contract I had with the museum for their new wing got canceled," Paul said. "I'm still not sure why. But it would have sustained me for almost a year. I don't want to speak ill of the dead, especially since there's suspicious circumstances, but I feel like Bart had it out for me."

Something didn't sound right about that. Paul seemed like an awfully nice person. And if he was a decent businessman, why would Bart do that?

Max sauntered over to join us, placed his front paws on the desk, and looked over the plans. He was ready for the meeting to begin.

"Well, it's lucky for us that happened. Otherwise we wouldn't be working with you for our project. Right, Chloe?" Mom asked.

Deep down Mom was a romantic at heart. With all of her husbands I felt like she was just looking for love. And now she was on a mission to find that for me. Mercy.

CHAPTER FIVE

Our little town library was anything but quiet this evening. The gathering place for tonight's bingo tournament teemed with people setting up the room. This event was one of the biggest moneymakers for the high school scholarships. Most of the proceeds went to seniors pursuing some type of education after high school. The tables were arranged in rows facing the front of the room, where the bingo caller would stand. A raised platform had been brought in. Behind the platform was a large board to display numbers as they were called. This was serious business.

Mom and I surveyed the room as we arrived. "Where would you like to sit?" I asked her.

She looked all around, assessing the choices for the best spot. "How about the second row, toward the middle aisle?"

"Sounds good. That way it will be easy for you to go collect your winnings."

She had her game face on. I knew bingo was a game of chance, but Mom still wanted to win, if only for bragging rights. We wove our way past all of the chairs to her prime location. "Let's put our stuff down to save our seats and go purchase our cards," she said.

Max jumped up into a chair and Mom and I put our purses down, one on each side of him. My boy loved number puzzles, and I just knew he would really enjoy playing bingo. We left him and went to the table on the side to load up on cards.

"Hi Victor," Mom said. "We'll take the maximum number of cards each."

Victor counted off twenty cards from the giant stacks in front of him. "Here you go," he said. "Good luck."

"We'll need twenty more," I said. "Max is playing tonight too." I gestured back toward our table location where Max was exhibiting his best manners.

Victor peered around me and frowned. "I don't understand," he said, and looked back and forth between Mom and me.

Explaining Max's number smarts to people always sent them off kilter. "Yes, he's playing tonight too," I said.

Victor tipped his head. "Really?"

I nodded.

Victor counted off twenty more cards and handed them to me, his eyebrows raised.

"I'm sorry about Bart," Mom said.

Victor's shoulders slumped. He opened his mouth and closed it again. His chin wavered. "Thank you," he whispered.

We grabbed three different-colored bingo daubers, one for each of us, and returned to our seats. I placed a pile of cards in front of Max and a pile in front of me.

Mom leaned over to me, past Max, and said, "I feel bad for Victor. He seemed to really care for Bart. Continuing on with the bingo tournament must be hard since it was something they always did together."

Bart and Victor had been dating for quite a few months. Mom had said they met soon after Bart arrived in town. Victor seemed a good match for Bart and seemed to get him, with Bart's sophisticated taste for the finer things.

"It is sad. Hopefully tonight will pick up his spirits a bit. This looks like a lot of fun," I said. "Do you want to grab some snacks before it begins?"

Max looked at me, inquiring about ginger treats. I rubbed his head. "Maybe later, boy."

"I'll just have water and maybe some popcorn," Mom said and sat down.

I headed to the snack table to get our goodies. The room filled quickly with the remaining participants. We were just about to the starting time. I returned to Mom and Max with our supplies and hunkered down for a night of bingo.

"Hi Aunt Chloe and Max and Grannie Mabel," Angela said. She was scooting behind our chairs to reach the end of the table and the last seat to Mom's right side.

"Hi dear. And don't call me Grannie. That makes me sounds old. Please call me Grandma Mabel if you have to use a title," Mom said. She had lined up four cards, ready for game one to begin.

Angela looked over her head at me and smirked. I returned the expression.

"Well hello, Mabel, and everyone." Donna made her way to the seat right in front of us.

Mom raised her head and continued arranging her cards. "Hello," she said.

Donna dropped her purse on the floor and started placing her cards in front of her, ready for battle. This was supposed to be for fun and to support the kids.

"Ladies and gentlemen, I want to welcome you to our annual bingo tournament for scholarships," Judy said. If anyone was born to be in front of a crowd, it was her. Even if she had no audience, I think she'd pontificate as if she did. "This is the best turnout we've ever had. I'm expecting this to be the largest amount of scholarships we're awarding to our dear children."

Max coughed, not something I had seen him do very often.

Judy stopped and glared at the source of the noise.

I snickered.

She turned her gaze back to the crowd. "Continuing on. Thank you for coming and good luck. I'm going to turn it over to Victor to let the games begin," Judy dramatically ended. She returned the microphone to the stand on the table for Victor's use in calling the numbers.

He stepped up, turning the bingo cage and said, "Get ready every-one."

Mom grabbed the dauber like she was arming for battle, elbow out, poised.

"First number. B nine," Victor said slowly, articulating every sylla-ble. "B nine," he repeated and placed the ball in the holder on the wall behind him.

Max tapped me on the arm. I looked over at his card and saw he had the number. I picked up his dauber and marked it. He smiled at me.

"Next number. I twenty-three," Victor spoke loudly into the microphone. "I twenty-three."

"C'mon," I heard Mom mumble, her head bowed over her cards, arm in the air with the dauber ready.

Victor continued announcing three more numbers when the first winner of the night shouted, "Bingo!"

Angela jumped up from her chair and speed walked to the front of the room. She handed Victor her card, he nodded, and reviewed the numbers. "We have our first winner, ladies and gentlemen."

Angela made eye contact with him again and smiled.

"Well, that couldn't have been any faster," Donna loudly said. "Five numbers?"

"That's all it takes," Angela said as she swiped by Donna on the return to her seat.

"OK, everyone. Let's get ready for round two," Victor said. We continued that way through round ten and to the intermission.

Max tapped me on the elbow several times throughout the games. But for only about half of those did he have a number on his card. Maybe it would take a few tournaments before he started to get the hang of it.

Donna turned around in her seat to chat Mom up during our break. "Mabel, I'm telling you, you would have loved that last cruise I went on. You should seriously think about going with me sometime."

Mom looked at me like Donna had just told her she had three heads. "I think Donna's right. You should do that, Mom. You work hard and you deserve it. With me here taking care of the hotel, you should take some time for yourself."

"Well, you're no help, Chloe. I'm not rich like you, Donna. I can't afford things like that big, fancy Gucci purse you have or going on cruises every other week," Mom replied.

Donna's hand dropped to her purse on the floor next to her. "I bought that with my gambling winnings. Just think about it, OK?" Donna asked.

Mom shrugged.

"We're going to get started again," Victor announced. "Please grab your seats,"

I positioned mine and Max's remaining cards. Even if we didn't win, it had been fun.

Victor called three more games, and Max continued to tap my arm. He was still about fifty-fifty having the correct number. I wasn't sure why he hadn't grasped the pattern. Maybe there were too many distractions. With only a few games left, Max tapped my arm again.

He turned in his seat and looked at me, straight on. He was trying to communicate something. I wish I understood his mannerisms as much as he understood mine.

I petted him. "What is it, boy?" I whispered.

He tapped his card. I pointed to one of the numbers. He nodded his head yes. I still didn't get it. He tapped me again and I pointed to another number. He nodded again. Now I was starting to catch on. Max had noticed a pattern where some numbers had never been called. Was he trying to tell me that he thought Victor was cheating? Why would Victor do that? Taking money from the scholarships? Max had to be mistaken. But how could I know for sure?

We were on the home stretch with the next-to-last game coming up. Max's accusation distracted me from daubing our cards. He continued to tap me, now more called numbers appearing on his card. With only one more number, G sixty, Max would have a bingo.

As if willing it, Victor called, "G sixty." He paused. "G sixty."

Max looked at me and began barking. My boy that had been silent as a mouse the entire time was now making a spectacle of himself. And rightly so. He had just won a bingo game. I daubed the last number, he grabbed the card, and trotted up to Victor, dropping it at his feet.

Victor picked it up by the corner and verified it was a winner. Everyone clapped, and Max turned and faced the audience, taking it all in. He leapt from the platform and sprinted back to his seat, ready for our last game.

We finished that last round without another win. But Max would ride that high from his victory for quite a while.

CHAPTER SIX

Max and I looked forward to a nice, relaxing stroll in the dog park. At least it would be relaxing for me. Every time Max came, he romped until his tongue almost touched the ground. I was glad to be able to bring him to a place to play with other dogs. He hung around me so much, he sometimes seemed more human than canine. Ever since the park had been built, it was a busy place. The setup provided a walking path around the fenced perimeter and lots of play space in the middle.

I leashed up Max as we exited the car until we got inside the park. We entered through the gate, I unleashed him, and he took off like a rocket, greeting his long-lost friends. The longer I was in town, the more I got reacquainted with people I hadn't seen in years, and the more new friends I made. I was sure I would see someone I knew at the park. I began my stroll and took in the gorgeous territorial views across the valley. The fresh air cleansed my lungs and cleared my head. I took a deep breath and thought about the events of the last few days. I needed some time to sort out what was going on with Bart's death. Still not much news from the Emerald Hills PD, either.

"Chloe, wait up, and I'll walk with you."

I turned around and saw Kathleen Timmons. She had just released her beagle into the play area. If I didn't have my cocker spaniel, I would definitely get a beagle. I waited for her to catch up. I hadn't known Kathleen before I moved back to Cedarbrook. She was Caroline's younger sister and always wanted to hang around with us in high school.

"It's nice to see you again," I said.

We began our walk around the path. "Likewise," she said.

We approached the corner, and I looked for Max in the pack of dogs to be sure everyone was behaving. There were a few tussles now and then, but mostly the dogs just chased each other. Many of the other owners brought toys and things to throw for their dogs, which gave everyone a workout.

"That was a lot of fun last night at bingo," I said. "It's heartwarming that this town does so much for their kids."

We kept to a leisurely stroll. "It really is. I was especially glad to see Angela win a few times. She needs the money, and I know it boosted her spirits after the disaster the other night at the museum," Kathleen said.

I looked at Kathleen. "You guys are friends, right?" I asked.

She smiled. "Yes, our daughters are the same age. We've almost been joined at the hip most of their lives," she said. "I just hope now that Bart's gone, the museum board does the right thing and hires her for the curator position. They should have done that in the first place. Bart didn't deserve that position." Kathleen no longer had a smile on her face. Her pace picked up, and I had to speed up to stay with her.

We rounded the farthest corner from the entry gate. I was glad I was on the inside of the track since it was a little shorter. Any faster and we would be at a jog. "You didn't like Bart?" I asked.

She looked at me, pressing her lips together. Practicing my detective skills, I let the uncomfortable silence stand.

She looked away, her voice deepening. "You could say that."

I waited. We walked the entire length of the park. She was apparently not going to offer anything else without prompting. "He seemed to be doing really well for the museum. I understand it was expanding and he'd been able to acquire some rare pieces for it."

Kathleen stopped, her fists balled. She tilted her head down. "Yeah, things are never what they seem," she said through gritted teeth. She turned and continued the fast pace. I was getting my workout in exchange for this conversation. But if it could provide me some insight into Bart, so be it.

"What do you mean?" I asked, hoping my open-ended questions would keep her talking.

She sighed. I thought this might be the end of this line of questioning. "There's that thing with Angela not getting the museum curator position. But I can't really fault him for that. Although, his shady dealings probably gave him a leg up on being selected. He and my brother were dating. I just didn't like how Victor behaved when it came to Bart. Their relationship seemed to change him, and not in a good way," she said. Her pace slowed a bit.

"I'm sorry." Thankfully, I was able to catch my breath enough to continue the conversation. "It's always tough when a family member makes choices you don't agree with, or that you don't think are in their best interest."

I searched the sea of dogs to make sure Max was still behaving himself. Alone with me, he was angelic. With other dogs? Sometimes that herd mentality got the better of him. I saw him chasing a poodle that looked exactly like a neighbor dog back home. Max and Bruce had become fast friends before we moved to Cedarbrook. Maybe someday we would pay a visit to reacquaint the two.

"Victor really fell hard and fast for Bart. I think he was blinded to Bart's ways. Victor was buying expensive things for Bart with money he didn't have. I don't know how he afforded it. I don't think the extra money he was getting from Angela renting a room was nearly enough to cover those pricey items..." she trailed off.

"I'm sorry, Kathleen. That must have been hard for you to be in the middle like that," I said.

"No matter how many times I tried to talk to him, Victor contradicted every one of my arguments," she said. "There was no cracking that thick skull."

Kathleen's beagle sprinted over to her and sat down, panting. We stopped. Kathleen crouched to pet her dog. I looked over at Max and he showed no signs of slowing down. Ultimately I would have to intervene.

"Eventually, I just had to bite my tongue. Even when I had evidence of Bart's cheating, Victor would have none of it," Kathleen said. She looked at me, sadness in her eyes.

"Sometimes people have to learn the hard way themselves. We just don't want to admit it, even when the truth is staring us in the face," I said.

She stood. "So true. And I wasn't the only one that saw it. It was a public place. I was at Caroline's where Bart was having coffee with Stan. They didn't seem to be trying to hide or anything," she said. "Of course, Bart denied it. Said they were talking business. Which I thought was a good cover story."

We had been at the park about an hour, enough time for Max to exhaust himself.

"I'm sad Bart's dead and that Victor is upset," she said. "But I'm not sad they aren't together anymore. That might make me a horrible person, but those are my feelings."

I called Max over and hooked the leash onto his harness. He obediently sat, ready to go. "I just hope we find out soon what happened so we can all have some peace," I said.

"Me too, Chloe," she replied.

"I'm glad we got to chat. I'll see you soon." I waved goodbye. Max and I made a beeline to the car, both a little wiped out. In his short amount of time in town, Bart had sure developed a complicated life.

CHAPTER SEVEN

The hotel office had started to look like a construction site. Plans were posted on the walls, supplies had been stored in the open spaces. We barely had a walkway to maneuver. I contemplated leaving the pups at Mom's while all of this was underway, but it was a lot of fun having them around.

Paul stopped in again for another update. The treehouses were taking shape, and the frame for the lodge was almost complete. The office door opened and a rush of cool air blew through. Trixie and Max sprinted to greet our guest. They both excitedly yipped and, completely forgoing any manners, jumped all over Paul.

He stopped with the door open, unable to proceed past the welcoming committee.

"Max. Trixie," I said. They completely ignored me and continued their routine. I strode toward the door and clapped my hands three times. Max turned and looked at me, knowing full well my message. Trixie, in her own world, as usual, jumped on Paul for his attention. "Trixie," I said, sternly. I grabbed her harness to disrupt her and let Paul all the way into the office.

He shook his head, a good sport about being mauled. "It could be worse. They might not like me and then we'd have a different scenario on our hands," he said. He closed the door and made his way over to the wall with the plans displayed. I let Trixie go. She and Max sprinted behind Paul. He now had a full entourage.

I followed them to the other side of the room. "Thanks for being so easygoing about it. They can be pretty well-behaved, until they're not. And then they completely lose all composure."

Mom had sauntered up beside me, ready for a status report on the building. "Hi Paul," she said sweetly, looking back and forth between Paul and me. She would not quit.

Paul removed his hat, a gentlemanly gesture. "Hello, Mabel," he said with a giant smile, not missing her intent one bit. Was he on board with this date thing?

This was all starting to be too much. I needed to stick to business, for now.

"I'm excited to share an update with you. Things are going very well," Paul continued.

Mom looked at him, almost glassy-eyed. I was sure there were visions of son-in-law dancing in her head. She looked at me. I completely avoided her eye contact.

Paul pointed to the plan for the Crocus Castle. "This is my favorite. With the A-frame structure, and the wall of windows facing west, the lucky guests in this unit will be able to watch sunsets while sipping a cocktail on the deck," he said.

Mom clasped her hands and held them up to her chin. "Oooo, that sounds so romantic."

I turned my body ever so slightly away from her to try and cut off that line of thinking. "How much longer before we can take a tour?" I asked.

Trixie barked sharply like someone had stepped on her foot. She sprinted toward the door and paced back and forth. I looked at Mom. "Can you hold her until we're done here?" At that moment, Max took off after Trixie, giving her reaction legitimacy.

Mom went to the window, stood on her tiptoes, and peeked out. "I think someone's here," she said. "But I don't see a car." She pulled the door open. Standing right on the other side was Donna with her arm raised as if she was going to knock. Who knocks at a place of business?

Donna lowered her arm and stepped into the office. "Hello, every-one," she said.

Mom closed the door and followed her. "Hi, Donna. What are you doing here?" Mom was nothing, if not to the point.

Donna approached Paul and said, "Hello, there. I'm Donna Sherman. And who are you?"

Paul reached out to shake her hand and said, "I'm Paul York. Nice to meet you."

Mom stepped into their sphere. "Donna, we're in the middle of something."

Donna continued gazing at Paul but acknowledged Mom. "Mabel, I came back to see if you had changed your mind about letting me buy some of your collectible pieces. With Bart no longer at the museum, I would be concerned about you letting that place have any of them."

Mom walked to the coffeemaker and over her shoulder said, "No, thanks. I don't trust anyone else with them." She got a tea bag, put it in a cup, and began filling it with hot water. She took a seat and held the cup, warming her hands.

"We'll let you know if we change our minds. Right now, Paul's plan is to create a beautiful display case in our new lodge to house the pieces," I said. I pointed to Donna's shoes where mud had crept up the sides. "I'm sorry it's so muddy here. I hope it didn't ruin your shoes."

Donna waved a dismissive hand and went to sit with Mom near the coffee pot. "Mabel, have you given any more thought to our conversation the other night at bingo?" Donna asked. "I just returned from a cruise to Alaska. It was spectacular. The views, the glaciers, the wild animals. And there's endless food and entertainment on the ship. You just have to come with me," she said.

Mom's eyes pleaded with me for an intervention. I actually agreed with Donna. Mom could use a break, and she might like a cruise.

"I would be too cold," Mom said to Donna.

Donna looked at me, enlisting my support. "There's other ones where it would be warm and tropical. Say you'll think about it, OK?" Donna asked.

Mom, seeing there was likely no other alternative to getting Donna out of here, agreed to consider it.

Donna jumped up, her large purse swinging to bonk Max on his snout. He barked, looked at me, and shook his head. Oblivious, Donna headed to the door. "Bye, all," she said and left.

Mom got up and joined Paul and me at the plans. "Ugh, that woman is so pushy. I don't know if I could be sequestered with her on a boat for that long."

Max was sniffing Donna's muddy footprints, bringing that to Mom's attention. "And look at the mess she made. I don't think she even wiped her feet," she said.

Um, thanks, Max. "Don't worry. I'll get that later," I said. I turned my attention to Paul. "When do you think we can tour the new units?"

He grinned from ear-to-ear. Yes, the entertainment here was frequent and free. "It shouldn't be too long now," he said.

Max entered the picture and stood right next to Paul.

Paul scratched Max's ears. Max closed his eyes and smiled. "He seems to like me. I hope that's a good sign," he said and looked at Mom. They connected with a conspiratorial look. "Well, I better head outside to check on the crew," he said.

Mom, the pups, and I escorted Paul to the door. As soon as it closed, Mom said, "Chloe, he would be perfect for you."

I hoped if I ignored her, she'd cease her matchmaking, but I was fooling myself. She couldn't help it. And Max had joined forces with her. I'd have to come up with some new avoidance strategies. Not that I wouldn't want to have a love in my life at some point. But just not right now. With Bart's murderer running loose in town, the hotel expansion, not to mention just the day-to-day running of the place, who had time for anything else?

CHAPTER EIGHT

"Mom, can you try to have an open mind about this?" I asked. Getting her to the travel agent's office was a herculean feat itself, let alone actually choosing a trip to go on. We pulled into the parking lot, I turned off the car and looked at her, waiting for a response. I was hopeful but not optimistic. I really wanted this for her sake. Max whimpered in the back seat. "See, Max thinks you should go too." I reached around and petted him.

Mom opened her door and got out. "Let's just see if Kathleen has anything I like and go from there," she said and closed her door.

Max and I looked at each other and shrugged. Yep, we never knew what to expect from Mabel.

We all headed into Kathleen's office to start the process. Two desks faced the entry doors. Travel posters of faraway places plastered the walls. Every type of location you could imagine was displayed in living color. Along the wall under the windows were several display cases of pamphlets. The visual barrage overwhelmed me. I didn't know how Mom would choose.

Kathleen got up from her desk and came to the other side to greet us. "Hello, everyone. I'm so glad you're here," she said. She gestured to two chairs facing her desk. She returned to her chair, placed her elbows on the desk, hands clasped, and leaned toward us. "So what can I help you with?" she asked.

I looked at Mom. Silence. She wasn't making this easy. Any other person would be jumping at the chance to escape. I looked back at Kathleen. "Mom is interested in exploring cruises," I said.

Kathleen looked at Mom. "OK, great," she replied. "Let's talk a little more about what you might like so I can narrow it down. Then I have some brochures you can look at," she said.

Mom held her purse on her lap like a shield. We waited. Finally, she blurted, "It can't be cold."

Kathleen's excellent customer service came through. "That's a great start," she said. "I have several tropical locations." She got up and gathered a stack of brochures from the racks near the window. She returned to her desk and fanned them out.

I scooted to the edge of my chair to get a better look. If Mom didn't end up going, maybe I would someday. "Do they have cruises where you can bring your dog?" I asked. Max leapt up and placed his snout on the edge of the desk.

Kathleen laughed. "Of course. They have cruises for just about everything and everyone."

I pulled one of the brochures to the edge of the desk in front of Mom. "OK. I'll come back another day to talk more about those. Mom, do you see anything you like?" I asked.

She leaned forward, glancing at the Caribbean pictures. "Hmm. That one does look nice," she said.

Oh, boy. Were we going to play twenty questions for which cruise to pick? "Kathleen, what has Donna done that she's liked?" I asked.

Mom looked at me, her lips pursed. "I probably won't like any of those."

Kathleen looked at Mom. "She's done almost everything. Cruises, bus trips, overseas travel. Her penchant is gambling and museums. So anywhere that takes her to a game of chance or a tour of collectibles, she's in." Kathleen pulled out a pen. "Why don't I show you these brochures one by one, and you can say yes or no. I'll make a list of the ones you like and get you more details on those so you can make a decision. How does that sound?"

No response from Mom. She really was making this difficult. Perhaps we would have to try again another day. "That's an unusual pen," I said, pointing to what Kathleen held in her hand.

She looked at it. "Victor got this for me. They had a limited number made at the museum the last time they had an unveiling with Bart." She paused and looked up. She swallowed and pulled out a pad of paper, then took a deep breath.

"I'm sorry," I said. I hadn't meant to open a wound.

"It's just so fresh," she said quietly. "Well, let's get started on a happier topic." She scooped all of the brochures into a pile and one by one placed them in front of Mom. Mom voted either yes or no, and Kathleen made two more piles. She obviously had experience guiding decisions with people too overwhelmed with all of the choices. I was impressed because Mom was not an easy customer. By the end of the pile Mom had selected four cruises as possibilities. Kathleen began to make a list and write some additional details. She retrieved a folder from her desk drawer and placed the brochures inside.

"Mom, some of those look really nice. I think you're going to enjoy the warmth and being pampered," I said. I hoped my encouragement would help convince her to do this.

"I don't need people to wait on me. I've worked hard all my life and never expected anything from others," she said. That woman was a tough nut to crack. If she wasn't ready, maybe I could convince her to go on a cruise with me. Or, if I could work miracles, maybe all of us triplets. Why not? I would just have to make sure the ship was big enough for us all to have our own space, when needed.

Max sat up and scooted closer to the desk. I wasn't sure what his objective was.

Kathleen continued gathering papers and placing them in the folder. "I'm sending with you a brochure for each trip and a sheet that has all of the pricing options and details. My notes here will be a summary," she said.

Max barked as softly as he could, went to the rack of brochures, pulled one out, and returned it to Kathleen's desk.

Mom came to the edge of her chair and peered over. "That one looks perfect, Max," Mom said. "I want to go to the Mexican Riviera."

Kathleen and I laughed. She got the detail sheet for Max's selection and put it in the folder with the others. "Why don't you take a couple of days and look these over? We can make an appointment for you to return and we can talk about next steps," Kathleen said. She handed Mom the folder.

"I'm ready, Chloe," Mom said.

I stood. "Let's get on Kathleen's calendar before we go," I said. "How about Friday at two p.m.?" I asked Mom.

She was already at the door. "OK, but I've already made up my mind. I want to do the trip that Max picked out," she said.

I turned and looked at Kathleen. "We'll plan to be here Friday at two if that works for you, and we can see about booking that cruise."

Kathleen escorted us to the door. "That sounds great. Thank you for coming in. And Mabel, I think you're going to have the time of your life. You might just get hooked on travel like Donna," she said.

Mom pushed open the door. Max and I followed.

"Thank you." I waved to Kathleen.

CHAPTER NINE

I looked forward to exploring our town's farmer's market today. Max and I would load up on goodies and I got to see my sister Zoe. She and her long-time boyfriend Eldon lived quite far away from town on a little farm that was off-grid. They would bring their haul into town and sell or trade for the supplies they needed. The last time Mom and I had visited Zoe, she had encouraged me to bring Max and stay with them a few days for a respite from the busy times at the hotel. I was getting closer to taking her up on it. Nothing to do and nature for a few days was just what the doctor ordered for Max and me.

The rows of booths lined the perimeter of the library parking lot. It was the largest location in town to be able to house the growing number of vendors. Zoe had a prime location in the middle of the line. The crowd size was growing, and Max and I had to weave through the flow of people to reach Zoe's booth. She was sandwiched between Caroline's Confections and a man that made fishing lures. The nearby lake and ocean fishing was a big industry.

Zoe beamed when she spotted us. That country air agreed with her. She always looked as relaxed as if she had been vacationing on a beach for a few weeks with umbrella drinks. She stepped out from behind the counter and held her arms wide. Max pushed passed me, stepped between us, and looked up at Zoe. "Well, yes. First things first," she said and bent down to embrace Max. They both closed their eyes as they hugged each other. Zoe stood and reached her arms toward me. "Hello, beautiful."

"We need to visit more often if this is how we're treated," I said.

She grabbed my hand and led me into her booth. She swept her arm along the boxes overflowing with every kind of fruit and vegetable we could ever want. "You have your pick of the crop," she said. "I'll get a box started for you." She pulled an empty box from the corner and started filling it with several things. She set it to the side and said, "Why don't you come back here when you're ready to go and pick this up?"

I hugged her. "Thank you, Zoe. That's so generous. What else do you recommend here?" I asked.

"Of course, my neighbor. Caroline has some new candies that she's trying out on us. Her niece is an apprentice at her shop. They melt in your mouth. You have to try them."

Max was snooping through all of Zoe's boxes of produce that were packed into the booth. Zoe got out a yellow squash and held it for him to sniff. He turned his nose up. *That's my boy, no veggies, but bring on the sweets.* I had to disguise healthy for him, but inevitably he picked out the vegetables he didn't like and left them in the bowl. He made his way to a corner box of a small, oblong watermelon. He sniffed and stepped back. He moved to the left side and sniffed again. He stopped for a moment of contemplation. He trotted to the opposite side and sniffed, then pawed it, leaving a little scrape mark on top. He waited. He pawed it again, and waited.

"He thinks it's an animal," I said. He had never seen a watermelon before. "Oh, Max." He looked at me and tipped his head, not sure why his new friend wasn't playing.

"So Zoe, I don't think you'll believe this. Mom and I went to the travel agent's office, and I think she might actually go on a cruise," I said.

"You're kidding! How did you manage that?" she asked. Another customer had arrived and chosen several items. Zoe packed them up and took their payment.

"It's not a done deal yet. I really hope she does," I said.

"That's going to mean you'll be even busier at the hotel. Are you able to handle that?" she asked.

I called Max from behind the counter. Enough of trying to get the watermelon to play with you. "It's only for a short amount of time. And she deserves it. She's worked hard her whole life."

Zoe continued helping customers as we talked. "I heard about the other night at the museum." She shook her head. "I feel so bad for Angela. Joey told me that Angela's a suspect. But we just don't see it."

I shook my head. "Me neither. I'll have to return to the museum and see what I can find out. It's baffled me so far."

"The guy in the booth next door is Bart and Victor's neighbor." Zoe came from around the table and stood inches away from me. She looked around. "He told me he overheard screaming and yelling one night recently, like they were arguing."

I took a step back. "Really?" I asked.

She looked around again and back at me. "Yes, exactly that. Sometimes guys gossip more than women," she said.

"Well, Victor seemed pretty shaken up about the death. I don't think you can fake emotions like he had," I said, remembering the look in his eyes that night at the bingo tournament.

"Maybe," Zoe said. "Something to check out, for sure."

I looked down the row of booths. "I thought I saw him here. Does he have a booth?"

"Yeah, he's somewhere down there. He creates beautiful pieces of art using different types of inlaid wood. I don't think he makes a lot of money with it though."

"Well, Max and I'll wander over there and check it out," I said. I leashed up Max to keep him close to me as we squeezed past the throngs. "We'll stop by on our way out."

Zoe waved and turned to help another customer.

I could see from quite a ways away that Victor had the three walls of his booth filled with the gorgeous designs, but no one was buying them. He spotted me and waved. I returned the gesture.

When we got within earshot, I said, "Hi, Victor."

"Hi, Chloe," he said.

"Your work is stunning."

He sighed. "Yes, I wish more people thought so. I get a lot of lookie loos, and people who say the same thing but don't put their money where their mouth is."

"Well, they're missing out," I said and looked straight into Victor's eyes. "I can't tell you again how sorry I am about Bart."

"I was hoping by coming today and doing something normal, I'd feel better." He bowed his head and shook it. "But I miss having him here with me. It's just not the same."

"I see that you do animals. Would you be able to do a custom piece of Max for me?" I asked.

Victor stepped out from behind the table and looked down at Max. He made a circle around him, evaluating his model. "Well, yes I could. If you get me a photo, that would be best," he said.

I smiled. I was happy to help out an artist. And his work was lovely. "Perfect. I'll be in touch."

"Thank you. And Chloe, thank you for looking into Bart's death. I really am not going to get a moment's peace until his killer is caught."

Max and I turned to retrace our steps to Zoe's booth, gather our box, and head out. Victor seemed genuinely sorrowful at Bart's death. Could he just be putting on a show? Time would tell.

CHAPTER TEN

The crime scene tape cordoning off the dead body and missing collectible was long gone. The only sound in the museum was hushed voices viewing the different displays. Angela had resumed tours while the mystery of her boss's death continued to loom large. Max and I sat on the bench in front of the location where the canteen was supposed to be. If Bart was killed here, I wanted to visualize how it had happened. That might guide me to where I should ask more questions.

Angela had sidled up to me. I jumped when she started talking. "I'm so sorry to startle you, Aunt Chloe," she said.

I stood up and faced her. "No worries. We're all on edge about this." I reached over and hugged her tight. Max jumped down, leaned up against Angela, and looked at her with love. I held her at arm's length and stared into her eyes. "How are you doing?" I asked.

She shrugged and slumped onto the bench. "OK, I guess. I'm so conflicted. I didn't really like Bart. But at the same time, I hope they will consider me for the curator position now that he's gone." She looked up at me, her eyes pleading.

Responding to her unasked question, I said, "I'm trying Angela. It's complicated. Eventually, we'll have answers. Just try to hang in there." I held out my hand. She grasped it and tipped her head down again, beginning to sob. I sat on the bench and put my arm around her.

Out of the corner of my eye, I saw Max slink over to the side table in the display location. He looked all around, in the corners, and then stood on his hind legs with his front feet on the counter. He looked at me, summoning my presence.

I released my arm from Angela and went to see what Max had discovered. At first it wasn't apparent what he saw. I looked at him and shrugged. "What is it?" I asked.

He tapped his paw on a space that, unless you looked closely, you wouldn't notice that it had less dust than the surrounding space. It looked like one of the candlestick holders in the row of six was missing.

I turned around and asked Angela, "How many candle holders should there be on this shelf?" I gestured toward the open space.

She got up from the bench and approached, her brow furrowed. She walked the length of the counter, looking at it from multiple angles. "That's really odd," she said. She moved a few of the other display items, searching for something that obviously wasn't there. She looked up at me and her hand flew to her mouth. "Chloe," was all she could squeak out.

Max got down from the counter and nodded. He had likely just discovered the potential murder weapon.

Angela's eyes darted from me to Max, and to the empty dust-free former location of the missing candlestick. "Let's not get ahead of ourselves," I said, trying to calm myself down as well. "Take a deep breath. I'll alert the police that we have a potential murder weapon. Angela, I need you to go throughout the museum and make sure it didn't make its way elsewhere, and that it is indeed missing."

Her hand dropped to her side and she nodded.

"We're still gathering information. OK?" I said.

She nodded again.

"Can I take a look at Bart's office? Maybe there's something else that might pop up there," I said.

She looked toward the museum entry to see a small group coming into the building. "I have to go, anyway. Yes, please help yourself. And let me know if you need anything else."

I reached down and patted Max, telling him what a great job he did. Now on to explore further.

Bart's office was in the farthest corner of the museum. It was a small eight by eight just big enough for a desk, chair, and filing cabinet. It was highly organized. Pencil holder, stapler, file folders aligned like soldiers. I scanned the area to see if anything felt out of place, perusing one corner at a time. I had hoped not to pry too much, but with everything put in its place, I'd have to scour through drawers. I stepped up to the desk and sat in the chair, again, taking it all in. I started by opening the top left drawer. Trying to disturb as little as possible, I gently lifted the stacks of papers out. I fanned through them to see if something caught my eye. I looked down at Max, and he shook his head.

We continued through the remaining drawers on the left side and moved to the right. Following the same pattern, there was absolutely nothing of interest to guide the investigation of Bart's murder any further. "I don't know, Max. It seems like we're missing something obvious." I opened the bottom right drawer, hoping this last stack of papers held the answers we needed. Or I would even take a clue to more questions, at this point. Something. I looked through each item, hopeful the prize would be at the very end. Nothing. I replaced the papers in the drawer and closed it up. I sat back in the chair, looking around.

Max whimpered. He tilted his head, laser-focused on that bottom right drawer.

"We already looked at that one, buddy," I said. I got up from the desk, ready to leave. Max wasn't budging. "I trust you. Obviously, I'm not having any luck. And you're already batting a thousand for clue discovery today," I said.

He tapped the drawer with his paw. I opened it and retrieved the stack of papers. I began reviewing each one and setting it to the side.

Max barked. He tapped the drawer again.

I returned my attention to the stack and continued moving one piece of paper at a time from right to left.

He bent over and pulled the handle open with his mouth. After the drawer was fully open, he stuck his head all the way in the back and pulled out some crumpled papers. I guess that's an advantage of being eighteen inches off the ground. You've got a great view from down there. He continued pulling out crumpled pieces of paper and placing them in a pile next to me.

I picked one up and pressed it out on the desktop. It was a letter between Bart and Donna. She was reminding them of their deal. With Donna's endorsement of Bart for the position of museum curator, he had agreed to acquire some rare pieces for her personal collection. Well, this certainly confirmed some of the rumors about his shady dealings, but it didn't point to a clue of who would murder him. I continued unfolding the smashed papers to find more letters and a travel brochure.

"Did you find anything useful?" Angela had come into the office.

I grabbed my chest. "You startled me again," I said. My heart raced and my head pounded as I tried to make sense of Max's brilliant discovery. I turned around in the chair to face her. "I'm not sure. Was Bart planning a trip?" I asked.

She came further into the office and picked up the brochure from the desk and looked at it. Then she looked at me. "Not that I know of."

I shoved the entire pile back into the drawer. No sense upsetting Angela any further until I knew for sure what was going on. I had several pieces but I didn't even know if they were to the same puzzle. Max and I had a lot more work to do.

CHAPTER ELEVEN

After our trip to the museum, I needed some time to allow the clues to percolate. I hoped the distraction of creating the decorations for the scholarship auction would be enough of a diversion for my brain. Mom had generously agreed to host the work party if I agreed to pick up the treats. Caroline's Confections and Coffee Shop was our go-to for anything sweet. And Max's favorite place to be spoiled. It bustled on a Friday night. We patiently waited our turn in line. Caroline's display of goodies had significantly grown. There were several new items I had not seen before.

"Hi Chloe," Caroline said as we approached the counter. "I have your box ready to go." She wiped her hands on her apron and turned to retrieve a large box from the back table. "I put a few extra of my newest creation. A cream-filled cupcake. I think it's going to be a big hit." She put the box next to the cash register.

"Thank you," I said. "And I haven't had anything here that hasn't been a hit."

Max knew exactly the routine he needed to perform in order to get a treat. He gently placed his nose on the counter and raised his eyebrows. Caroline came out from behind the displays and placed a treat for Max on the floor. He gently grabbed it with as much politeness as possible, dropped it on the floor, and looked up at me, then Caroline.

She laughed and patted his head. "No fooling him," she said. "I tried a small piece of my new cupcakes, but as always, he's got his heart set on the gingersnaps." She pulled another treat from her apron pocket and placed it on the floor.

He inhaled it and looked up for another.

She held both hands up and rubbed them together to show him there was no more for today.

He tipped his head and returned to my side.

"Chloe, any further progress on Bart's murder?" Caroline asked, and returned to the other side of the counter.

I shook my head. "I wish. It seems the more I ask around, the more complicated it gets. Angela is beside herself that she didn't have anything to do with it. I want to believe her because she's family. But she sure did have a lot of motive. And she was there early the night of the museum unveiling."

"And she's got that sweet daughter too." Caroline packed up additional boxes for more pick-up orders. "Yeah, I can't see it," she said.

"The one I really don't know about is Victor. He and Bart had been overheard in a fight. Couples fight and they normally don't kill each other. But sometimes they do." I grabbed the box of pastries. "We'll just have to keep at it. Thank you for these. Let's go, Max."

He turned to look at me and then back at Caroline.

She put her hand up to the side of her mouth and whispered, "I put a few for him in the box."

I turned and almost smashed my box into the man behind me. "Oh, I'm sorry," I said. "I didn't realize there was anyone behind me."

He stepped to the side to let me pass before I made a total mess of the place. "No worries. Hi Caroline," he said.

"Hi Stan. Have you met Chloe yet?" Caroline asked and pointed my direction.

He bent to give Max's ears a scratch, which prompted a relaxed, happy smile from my pooch. "No, I haven't," he said. "I'd shake your hand, but I don't want to give you another chance to spill your box." He laughed and Max barked. "I think your friend likes me. I'm Stan

York. My brother Paul is doing the construction project at the hotel," he said.

I nodded and gazed at him, seeing a small likeness to Paul. "Ah, OK. Nice to meet you, Stan," I said.

He took a step back. "I won't keep you. I just want to say thank you for Paul's business, which I'm sure he's also said. Ever since Bart canceled our business with the museum, we've both been struggling."

"What do you do?" I asked.

"I'm a party planner. With all of the museum celebrations going on, Bart had been keeping me pretty busy. And after that, Victor canceled the contract for the scholarship presentation. If you or Caroline know of anyone that could use some catering and planning expertise, I'd be forever grateful," Stan said. "I better let you go. Nice to meet you again."

"You too," I said. Max and I turned and headed out the door. Why would Bart and Victor cancel the contracts? Stan and Paul seemed nice enough. And I'm guessing the work was decent. Another direction to pursue for answers.

❧

Donna, Kathleen, and Angela had already arrived at Mom's. We had planned a work session to create all of the decorations for the scholarship presentations happening the next evening. Trixie was already yipping to greet us, mostly Max. She adored him like an older brother. She also pestered him like a little sister. He was a good sport about it and tolerated her tugging his long ears, poking his rear, and generally annoying him. They would get on a roll sometimes and speed around Mom's house like a racetrack.

We entered the house, greeted everyone, and I took the box to the kitchen. I joined the work group in the dining room. Streamers, balloons, posters, and table decorations were spread out on every surface.

"Thank you for bringing those," Mom said.

I took a seat at the table to join the assembly line. "Of course," I said. "Caroline said she put in a few of the new cream-filled cupcakes she made."

"Chloe, why don't you put together the centerpieces?" Mom asked. "We have one here as an example, if you want to do that."

"Mom, I met Paul's brother when I was at Caroline's," I said. I placed seven small bottles in front of me. I grabbed a box with ribbon, glitter, and several sticks with the word "Celebrate" on them. I looked at the example and began assembling the first bottle.

"Stan is so nice," Kathleen said. "I really wish he and Victor had gotten together. But for some reason, Stan also wanted to date Bart."

Kathleen was making table cards and had several stacks already completed.

Max and Trixie had exhausted themselves and joined our work party, plopping down under the dining room table.

"So Donna," Mom began. I looked up at her. She continued her focus on the task in front of her. "I went to see Kathleen. And I think I might go on a cruise with you."

Donna squealed like a little girl. She gave a quiet golf clap. "Mabel, you won't regret it," she said. She sat forward in her chair, waiting for the answer.

Mom continued her task. "Mexico," she said.

More clapping from Donna. "That's fantastic!" She suddenly halted her euphoria and began looking around. "What's that noise?"

We all stopped our work and listened. From under the table came the sound of paper rattling. I thought someone likely had dropped some supplies that the dogs had gotten hold of. I peered under the table and saw Max unwrapping a butterscotch candy. "Oh, Donna. I'm sorry. It looks like Max got into your purse and snuck a candy. He has a relentless sweet tooth," I said.

Donna hauled her bag from under the table and lofted it onto the kitchen counter.

Mom peeked at me and snickered. I couldn't make eye contact with her or I would bust a gut. I'd give just about anything to be a fly on the wall during their cruise. There would be no end to the stories Mom would have when she returned. I couldn't wait.

CHAPTER TWELVE

The layout of the library looked identical to what it was on bingo night. Tables faced the front platform where the presentations would occur. The decorations we had created provided a lovely, festive atmosphere. It would be a wonderful celebration of the graduating high school seniors and a hearty send off for the next phase of their lives.

Mom, Max, and I made our way to the same seats we had during bingo. Each table had several decorations, including blank cards. We were all encouraged to write notes of inspiration to the seniors. The tables quickly filled in with friends and family of the graduates. I looked over the program that had been placed in front of each chair. There would be opening remarks from Judy, of course. Then interspersed, we would be treated to seniors performing in different arts, as well as the scholarship and awards presentations themselves. What a joyous night and a nice break from the stress of the recent tragedy.

"Good evening, everyone." Judy had stepped to the podium to kick us off. "If you will take a seat, we are just about to get started. Thank you," she said. She huddled up with Victor and the high school principal, Mrs. Hardcastle, to review the itinerary. Judy nodded as she reviewed the paper in front of her. She looked at the clock on the wall and returned to the microphone. Victor and Mrs. Hardcastle each took a seat behind Judy on the platform.

"I'd like to welcome you to one of my most cherished events to attend as the mayor of Cedarbrook," Judy began. She scanned the room, taking it all in. After a dramatic pause, she continued, "Tonight we get to celebrate the next class of high school graduates. Please join me in acknowledging their accomplishments." She put her paper down and led us in a round of applause. "And if that wasn't enough, this will be the largest dollar amount of scholarships we've ever given." She grinned big as if she had personally donated the funds. She panned the crowd again.

At that moment, Victor rose and approached Judy's right side, and with a hand to his mouth, whispered in her ear. He dropped his hand and took a step back.

"Are you sure?" Judy asked in a loud whisper. She looked back at the crowd. Her mouth opened and closed without a word. She shook her head. "I'm sorry. I have some disappointing news. I have just been told by the bingo treasurer that we do not, in fact, have the amount of money to award scholarships as I was previously advised."

Victor took another step back toward his chair.

Judy turned to her right, grabbed his arm, and pulled him to the microphone. "You need to tell them how much we have and where the money has gone." She made space for him to address the crowd. A significant amount of mumbling had begun.

From across the room, one of the parents shot out of their seat and yelled, "Where's the money?"

A smattering of other parents stood and another one yelled, "Thief. I think he should be arrested. Call the police."

Victor took a step back from the podium and held his arms up, trying to halt the mob's ire. "Wait a minute. Let me explain," he said.

Those that were standing took their seats. But the low-level grumbling continued.

Victor's shoulders rose and fell. "Yes. I admit it. The funds are not currently there," he said.

The yelling began again, up another octave. Mom leaned over to me and whispered, "This better be good." I agreed. Victor had quite the hole to dig out of, and I didn't see any way he could recover.

"Where are they?" came another shout.

Victor looked at Judy, pleading for her to create some order. She took a step back, leaving him in the arena to fight this out alone.

"He was going to pay them back. I promise. It was just a temporary loan. Bart said no one had to know," Victor said. He voice shook, now caught in the web of deceit.

"Liar," came an accusation from the crowd. "You've been spending a lot of money you don't normally have. Explain that."

Victor shook his head and brought a fist up to his mouth to stifle sobs. He returned to his seat without another word.

Judy returned to the podium and resumed control. She sneered at Victor as he passed by her, and rightly so.

"Well, we're going to have to change up our program tonight. One way or another we will find a way to award the amount in scholarships that was promised," Judy said.

A huge cheer and round of applause roared from the crowd.

Judy beamed. "Before we continue, I'd like to assure you there will be a full accounting of the funds. Victor will no longer manage the books. We'll have a professional look at them from now on," Judy said.

Another huge round of applause and cheers emanated throughout the library, echoing off the walls.

Judy pointed toward me. "I'm sorry to put you on the spot. But, Chloe, would you please take a look at the books and let us know what's really going on?" Judy asked.

What could I say? "Of course. I'd be happy to." Maybe I would get Max to buddy up with me for the task. Together we had become an unbeatable team. I looked over at Max seated between Mom and me. He nodded.

More cheers and calls of "thank you, Chloe" came from the crowd. I smiled, happy to help with anything for the kids. The program for the night continued on, albeit a small deviation from the original plans. The joy of the evening with the smiles on those senior's faces helped us all recover from an inauspicious start to the night. As the evening was wrapping up, Judy reminded everyone to fill out the cards on our tables with words of encouragement for the seniors.

"Chloe, do you have a pen I could borrow?" Mom asked. That woman had the kitchen sink in her purse. How could she not have a pen? I traveled light with a small carry-all just big enough for ID, keys, and money.

"I have one," Angela said as she dug in her purse. She turned and held it out for Mom to take. Max intercepted it just as Mom's hand stretched to take it.

"Max," Mom said. "Give me that."

He clamped down hard, not giving it up. He turned toward me in his chair. I reached to take it out of his mouth and saw the same museum collectible pen Kathleen had at her office. He released it into my hand and looked me straight in the eye. I nodded to acknowledge his message and retrieved the pen for Mom. Was this another piece to the puzzle we were looking for?

CHAPTER THIRTEEN

Paul had arrived for another walkthrough of the hotel expansion project. The Crocus Castle was almost complete and we would get our first look from the inside of the treehouse. Thankfully, Paul had recommended an elevator for this unit. As our tallest building, it warranted an easier lift. Mom, Paul, Max, and I made our way along the path to the farthest location from the office and new lodge. The ground had dried up from a recent rain but remained a bit soft. I would have to remember to ask Paul to firm up the path to this unit with some wood shavings to prevent any slips and falls.

"Be careful, Mom. It's still a bit soft," I said. Thankfully, she relented to wearing a pair of hiking boots I had purchased for her. Those dress shoes she always insisted on wearing were going to land her in a puddle, or worse. I grabbed her hand, just to be safe. We approached the base of the ponderosa pine tree that was the foundation for Crocus Castle. It had grown to a width of almost twenty feet, approaching its size at maturity. Looking up, we could only see the bottom of the wrap-around deck that enveloped the treehouse. The elevator would take us through that and open just outside the front door. My heart palpitated.

"Chloe, why don't I take Mabel up first? Then I'll come back to get you and Max," Paul said.

"Oh, goody," Mom squealed like a giddy schoolgirl. This project for the hotel was making her dream come true. A real legacy left to her recent husband. She had been wanting to do this for so long. I was so pleased I could help make it happen for her.

Paul loaded Mom into the elevator and they slowly lifted off. It was actually quieter than I expected, retaining the tranquility of its surroundings.

Max and I patiently waited for Paul's return. Just as slowly, he descended and opened the gate for us to enter. I looked around and estimated probably four people at the most could fit into this space.

Paul looked over at me and asked, "What do you think?"

"I think it's incredible. Better than I ever imagined," I said.

"Wait until you see the view. I don't want to ruin the surprise for you. But it's spectacular," he said. His excitement was infectious. I bet it was so rewarding to delight your customers with results beyond their wildest dreams.

The elevator came to a halt and Max sped to the opening, anxious to escape. I hadn't even thought about his reaction to that new experience. I hoped it didn't frighten him. He ran down the decking to greet Mom, who stood in the northwest corner taking in the view.

"Chloe, look." She gestured to the tops of the trees as far as the eye could see.

I stopped. My breath, literally taken away. Other than being in an airplane, this was not a view most people would ever see. My marketing brain hummed with ideas for aerial photos. We would have to do it up right for the brochures and website. I continued along the deck toward Mom. "I can just see chairs and a table out here for watching the sunset," I said. "Wow."

Paul chuckled behind us. "I'm guessing you like it so far."

I looked over my shoulder. "It's breathtaking."

Mom pointed to something in the distance. "I can see forever. Look, someone's coming up the road to the hotel." We still had a gravel road to the hotel for the short distance from the main paved highway. It got a little messy during the wet winters.

I stood closer to Mom. "I think that's Donna's car," I said. "We should probably head back to the office. Thanks so much for the tour."

"My pleasure." Paul headed toward the elevator. "Any time. Let's do the same plan as we did when we came up."

Mom got into the elevator with Paul, which left Max and I to wait our turn. When we were all on the ground again, we trekked back to the office.

"That was great, huh Mom?" I asked.

Max took off, sprinting toward Donna. I wasn't sure why he didn't seem friendly toward her, but he must have had a good reason.

We exited the path into the parking lot. Donna had disappeared. "Where did she go?" Mom asked.

"Maybe she went inside," I said. "C'mon Max," I yelled. We turned and headed to the office door.

Max yelped like he had injured himself. I turned around and Donna appeared from the other side of her car. I walked toward her to locate Max. "Hi, Donna. We thought you had already gone inside."

She briskly walked past Mom and me and opened the office door. Over her shoulder she said, "Oh, I dropped something. But I want to talk to you both about a brainstorm I had."

Mom looked at me, shrugged, and followed Donna inside.

I went to investigate what was happening with Max. He emerged from the bushes on the side of the parking lot, limping. Oh no. Every now and then he strained one thing or another after his jaunts. Like a fine-tuned athlete, he periodically needed physical therapy. That usually meant a relaxing massage at Pearl's Pooch Pampering. He stopped where he was and waited. He held his left front paw a few inches from the ground.

"What happened, Max?" I asked. I bent over and began to gently feel up and down his leg to locate the source of the injury. He didn't flinch once. Instead, he held his leg higher so I could see the bottom of his foot. Stuck to his paw was a butterscotch candy. I carefully peeled it off so he could at least walk on it again.

"Max, that sweet tooth is going to get you into deep trouble one of these days," I said. I placed his paw on the ground and headed toward the office. I turned around and saw he hadn't moved from his spot. I walked back toward him and he dove into the bushes. The squirrels had been extremely busy lately, burying food for the winter. Maybe he had located part of their stash. He poked his head out to confirm I was coming and returned into the bushes. OK. I was going to have to follow him to resolve whatever it was he wanted me to see. I parted the branches and followed the sound of rustling.

About six feet in, I saw what he had found. The missing canteen and candlestick holder from the museum. Someone had stashed them in the bushes. I followed him all the way in and picked up the items that were damp from the rains. If not for Max, I don't know that they would have been located for quite a while, if ever.

We wove our way out of the bushes, across the parking lot, and into the office.

CHAPTER FOURTEEN

As I approached the office door, I spotted Paul coming this way. "Chloe, if you have a few minutes, I have some questions for you and Mabel," he said.

I nodded and slowly opened the office door. Max sprinted past me. I held the door open for Paul and stepped inside.

"Oh, good, Chloe. Donna has a great idea, she wanted—" Mom's jaw dropped open and she stood up. She and Donna had settled into the chairs near the coffee pot. Mom took a step toward me. "What is that? Where did you get it?" she asked.

Max had run to Donna and was now in a tussle with her for her purse. She yanked it hard, but he had a death grip, and there was no way that elderly lady would win that battle. He growled and bared his teeth. She stood and Max tugged hard. Donna lost her balance and the contents of her purse tumbled out, making a pile about a foot tall. At the top of the mound was a giant bag of butterscotch candies.

"Make him stop," Donna screamed.

I stepped further into the office and held out the canteen and candlestick, one in each hand. "Was this what you were looking for in the bushes?" I asked.

"I don't know what you're talking about," Donna said and crossed her arms over her chest. "I came to ask you about hosting a casino night at the new lodge. But this is the thanks I get for trying to help your business?" She stooped and began shoveling the pile of items back into her bag.

Max returned and grabbed the handles of her purse, dragging it to the opposite side of the room.

Donna grabbed her wallet and keys and stood up. "See if I ever help you again. And Mabel? That cruise is off!" Donna yelled and started toward the door.

Paul stepped in front of her, preventing the exit. I didn't think he fully understood what was happening, only that Donna shouldn't be allowed to leave just yet.

"Get out of my way, you big oaf!" Donna tried to skirt around Paul, but he stepped into her path.

I put the canteen and candlestick on the counter and wiped my grimy hands on a towel. "Donna," I uttered quietly, trying to defuse the situation. "I read the letters between you and Bart. I know you were blackmailing him to get those museum pieces for your personal collection." I took a small step toward her. I kept my voice low. "And your muddy shoes from the other day were because you were trying to find where you had ditched the items the previous time you were here," I said.

She turned toward me. "Bart was always so full of himself. He wouldn't have had that position if it weren't for me. I knew more about collectibles than he ever would," she said. Her chin trembled. Her arms went limp.

I took a step toward her. "What happened, Donna?"

She looked at me and we both shuffled back toward the chairs. I continued in lockstep to keep her moving. I gestured to the chair. She sat, bent over, and began weeping into her hands.

Paul brought over a box of tissues, and I handed them to Donna. I made the signal and mouthed to Paul to call the police. He nodded. I needed to keep Donna talking until they arrived. "It's all over, Donna," I said.

Mom joined the conversation after the shock of the situation had dissipated. "Now what am I going to do? I've already put down a deposit on that cruise that's non-refundable," she said. She sat down in a huff next to Donna.

I stood guard. "We'll figure something out, Mom. Don't worry. I'm sure Kathleen can help us," I said.

Max joined us, still dragging Donna's empty purse like a prized catch, prancing to Mom's side. He whimpered, dropped the purse, and looked up at Mom. She reached down and patted his head.

"I'm so sorry, Mabel," Donna said, looking at Mom with pleading eyes.

"You should be apologizing for Bart," Mom said.

Donna took a handful of tissues and dabbed her drippy eyes and nose. "Mabel, I don't know what'll happen to my collection."

Mom stood, faced Donna, and jammed her hands onto her hips. "That's what got you into this pickle in the first place, your obsession with those things. And your collection isn't nearly as nice as all of the pieces we have here." Mom was not relenting.

Donna pleaded with Mom. "I know. That's why I want you to take care of what I have. Mabel, you and your family care as much about the history of Cedarbrook as anyone. I can't think of a better home for my babies until I can see them again."

Mom scoffed. "You got that right," she said and walked over to Paul. "Paul, do you think we could expand the plans for the display case we had?" she asked.

"Of course, Mabel. Anything for you," he said.

Mom strutted back to Donna and said, "There. All taken care of. Donna, if you weren't so full of yourself, maybe this wouldn't have happened. Your gambling habit just went too far this time. And poor Bart had to pay the price." Mom read her the riot act. It was reminiscent of the scolding we kids used to get at home. Donna would probably be relieved when the police came to take her away. She slumped further into the chair.

Max tiptoed to the pile of Donna's purse contents, trying to go unnoticed. He poked his nose searching for treats. "Max," I whispered. He paused, then continued prodding. "Max," I repeated.

I grabbed the purse and loaded the stuff back inside. He deserved the biggest gingersnaps I could find. It might take a special order at Caroline's to make him all that he should get for finally cracking this case wide open. He looked up at me, as if reading my mind, and smiled from ear to ear. His little tail took off again like that helicopter, happy for a job well done.

CHAPTER FIFTEEN

We were finally at the stage of the hotel construction project where we were confident enough to plan the grand re-opening. I was always in favor of going to the experts for help for things I don't know. Today, Mom, Max, Stan, Caroline, and I were all in the back room at Caroline's Confections. Caroline had set out samples of all the treats we might order for the event. Four tables were covered with every kind of sweet you could imagine, many I had never seen in her display cases.

"Caroline, you have really outdone yourself. This looks incredible," I said as I toured the tables. "How will we be able to narrow it down?" I laughed. We all circled the desserts several times and then gathered at a table to commence the planning.

Stan sat between Mom and me. He reached out a hand to each of us and looked back and forth. His voice cracked. "Chloe and Mabel, how can I ever pay you back with my gratitude? I owe you for so many things," he said.

I smiled. "I'm just glad we found you to help us plan this shindig. We want to do it up right," I said. Stan's party-planning business had begun to recover. The contract for the bingo games had even been restored.

He released our hands and opened the notebook in front of him. "Well, then you've come to the right place. Caroline and I will knock it out of the park. This town owes you for solving Bart's murder and finding the missing museum piece, even if it was damaged," he said.

"That Bart was a scoundrel," Mom interjected.

Max jumped up and started barking. He sauntered over to Caroline and placed his head on her thigh, opening his eyes wide. The two of them had become thick as thieves.

Caroline looked at me for permission. "He can have whatever he wants," I said. "If he hadn't been nosing around those bushes and got that candy stuck to the bottom of his paw, we might still be trying to figure out what happened."

Caroline knew Max well and always treated him right. She had a plate of his favorite gingersnaps in the middle of the table. She retrieved one, showed it to him, and tossed it up. He caught it mid-air, like the well-tuned athlete he was. He sat and stared at her, encouraging her to keep them coming. "OK, boy. Let's pace ourselves. We've got a lot to cover in our meeting," Caroline said and turned back to our planning committee. Max laid down beside her, still fixated on her hand the moment it had another treat inside of it.

"I'm still shocked that Donna did it." Mom joined the conversation. "I mean, she's a little old lady," she said. Mom didn't think of herself as a little old lady. That was partially why she was still able to help run the hotel at age eighty.

"I don't think she planned it. Since she used that candlestick to bonk him on the head, I'm guessing it just happened in the heat of the moment. Even so, she's still guilty," I said.

"It's still really sad. Bart didn't deserve that," Caroline said.

"Well, at least Angela was able to bail them out at the museum. That girl knows her history." Mom huffed. "She should have gotten the position in the first place."

The museum board, minus Donna, unanimously voted to hire Angela as the curator. She got the same compensation deal as Bart. The more business she brought in, the higher percent of commission she would earn. She had already planned the events for the next year, outdoing Bart. Plus, I think her infectious personality and authenticity drew people to the place. It has gotten to be one of the busiest locations in town.

So many people's lives had been upended because of Donna's deed. I hoped now that she had been caught, we could begin to heal. With Angela moving out of Victor's, he had moved in with his sister, Kathleen. The judge gave him community service hours for being complicit in taking the bingo money. He seemed repentant and was trying to build up his art business.

Caroline got up and handed out plates to everyone. "Why don't we sample these as we're doing our planning?" she asked. "There's a lot to try."

She must have prepared at least twenty-five different items. We all got up and shopped around to choose a few to begin our tasting. When we resumed our seats, Max circled the tables several times, waiting for his share of the goodies. Caroline place two more gingersnaps on a napkin and put it on the floor. Max inhaled those and looked around for the next course of his meal.

"That's enough for now, Max." He dutifully laid down. "Caroline, these truffles melt in your mouth," I said with my mouthful. "And the little crunch inside is delicious."

"Those are the newest creation. My niece Haley is an apprentice with me for the next year. She's really brought a lot of new ideas from her training at the culinary institute," she said.

I plopped another truffle in my mouth. "Your generosity to make up for the stolen bingo money was above and beyond."

"Well, with my business doing so well," Caroline said, "I wanted to give back. There was a time I wasn't sure I would be able to continue. But thanks to everyone rallying around me, we're finally operating in the black."

"I'm sure those students and their parents are extremely grateful," I said.

"Mmmmm," Mom mumbled. I looked over and her entire plate was empty. Stan, Caroline, and I looked at each other and smirked. "What?" Mom asked. "Caroline said to try them. I'm just following instructions." She got up to refill her plate. She returned to the table and said, "I hope this celebration will be one that people talk about for a long time." Mom looked at me. "Chloe, did you tell them?"

I held my hands up. "I thought you should be the one to share the good news," I said.

Caroline and Stan looked at each other.

"Does this mean—" Stan started. He covered his mouth.

"No, Stan. I'm still working on that," Mom said. "Chloe just doesn't know it yet."

I picked up a cookie and took a bite, averting my eyes from everyone. "Mom, stop trying to fix me up. When I'm good and ready, I'll search for a boyfriend by myself." My cheeks were on fire.

"Harrison and his family are coming for a visit when we have the grand re-opening. I get to see my son and have my family together again," Mom said. She beamed. This had been her wish for so long.

Caroline reached out a hand. "Mabel, I'm so happy for you."

"That's wonderful," Stan chimed in. "Now I get to do my job and make this an epic party." He looked at me and winked. "And Mabel, you and I will strategize later."

"Yes, we will, Stan," Mom said.

Max returned to the conversation, barking and wagging his tail. It would be an epic party, indeed.

HEAR FROM MAX

Max tells his side of the story. Scan the QR code below with your device's camera to find out the scoop straight from the pooch's mouth.

NEXT RELEASE - MISTLETOE AND MISFORTUNE

E pic plans are underway to celebrate the hotel's glorious expansion. But the untimely death of a pompous chef right in the middle of the preparations might be what closes down the hotel for good. Ben's award-winning restaurant and food are legendary, but not as much as his arrogance and unscrupulous dealings.

As Chloe and Max work to salvage the event, they discover secrets about the chef that will crack the case wide open. When Ben's wife takes the helm of the business with suspiciously no remorse for his death, she jumps to the top of the list of suspects.

The shocking clues that come to light will entangle Chloe's family, her mother's livelihood, and culminate with a bombshell that will leave everyone dumbfounded. Can Chloe and Max connect the dots in this culinary conundrum before the hotel doors are shuttered forever in *Mistletoe and Misfortune*?

Scan the QR code below with your device's camera to order now.

THANK YOU

Thank you for reading ***Buttercups and Betrayal.*** Reviews are crucial for helping other readers discover new books.. If you want to share your love for this book, please leave a review for other readers. I'd really appreciate it!

Scan the QR code below with your device's camera to leave a review.

About the Author

Sue Hollowell is a wife and empty nester with a lot of mom left over. Not far from her everyday thoughts are dreams of visiting tropical locations. She likes cake and the more frosting the better!
Scan the QR code below with your device's camera to follow her author page on Facebook.

www.ingramcontent.com/pod-product-compliance
Lightning Source LLC
Chambersburg PA
CBHW020739160726
47993CB00006B/2527